Wake Up, Lil Miss New York

LISA THOMAS

ISBN 978-1-64191-524-3 (paperback)
ISBN 978-1-64299-739-2 (hardcover)
ISBN 978-1-64191-525-0 (digital)

Christian Faith Publishing, Inc.
832 Park Avenue
Meadville, PA 16335
www.christianfaithpublishing.com

Printed in the United States of America

For Dave, Alissa and Carlita - The Loves of my life

Here I am! In your face!
Blazing brightly, no need to wait!
Wake up, Lil Miss New York!

You can't hide from the light,
it's time for you to take flight!
Like the birds in the sky
and the beautiful butterflies.
Wake up, Lil Miss New York!

Roll to the left, roll to the right,
twisting all around,
This is about to be a pillow fight!
Wake up, Lil Miss New York!

Cold floor beneath your feet,
as you try and hop out of bed
from under your daisy printed,
soft purple sheets.
Wake up, Lil Miss New York!

9

There are so many exciting things to do
in a city that is waiting just for you!
Wake up, Lil Miss New York!

Concrete under your feet,
headed to the pizza shop
or corner store for a lunchtime treat.
Wake up, Lil Miss New York!

13

Museums full of history,
the thrilling ride on a crowded subway train,
the subway singers and dancers that entertain!
Wake up, Lil Miss New York!

Can you hear my rhythm?
The rhythm in my sound
of the city, echoing all around?
Fire trucks' sirens, city cabs' horns honking,
whistles blowing, garbage trucks squeaking,
dogs barking, and birds chirping?
Wake up, Lil Miss New York!

Can you smell the sizzling bacon, coffee brewing, and mom's perfume drifting through the air?

Wake up, Lil Miss New York!

There you are! I can hear your footsteps, I can see your face, a great big smile, and you're wide-awake!

About the Author

The author is a native New Yorker with a huge heart for children of all ages. She attended Long Island University, where she studied psychology and social work. The author has spent most of her life introducing students to the world of education as an early childhood and kindergarten teacher. Her love for children and her ability to mold young minds has been one very significant highlight in her life. Her drive has always been to unlock every child's door to their imagination and make learning fun. Throughout her career in teaching she has learned the keys to motivating and helping her students discover their gifts and abilities.

The author and her husband share their home in Northern Virginia with their two extraordinary daughters and a lifetime collection of books. She writes about her experiences growing up in New York. A city full of excitement and adventure. She writes about going through life as a child in the city. Through her writing she wants children to be inspired and empowered.

9 781642 997392

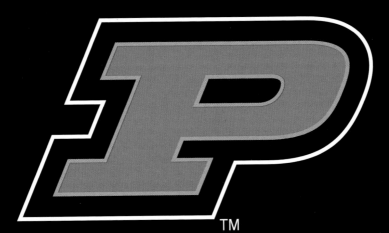

Hello, Purdue Pete!

Aimee Aryal

Illustrated by Julie Reynolds

www.mascotbooks.com

It was a beautiful fall day at
Purdue University.

Purdue Pete was on his way to
Ross-Ade Stadium
to watch a football game.

He walked across Purdue Mall and
stopped in front of Hovde Hall.

A professor passing by waved
and said, "Hello, Purdue Pete!"

Purdue Pete strolled past
the Bell Tower.

A couple walking by said,
"Hello, Purdue Pete!"

Purdue Pete walked through
Memorial Mall.

A group of students studying near the fountain said, "Hello, Purdue Pete!"

Purdue Pete made his way to
Purdue Memorial Union.

A girl walking down the steps yelled,
"Hello, Purdue Pete!"

It was almost time for the football game. As Purdue Pete walked over to the stadium, he passed by some alumni.

The alumni remembered Purdue Pete
from their days at Purdue. They said,
"Hello, again, Purdue Pete!"

Finally, Purdue Pete made his
grand entrance at the stadium.

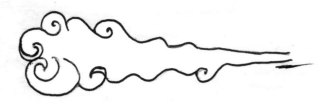

As he rode onto the football field
in the Boilermaker Special,
the crowd cheered, "Go, Purdue!"

Purdue Pete watched the game
from the sidelines and cheered
for the home team.

The Boilermakers scored six points!
The quarterback shouted,
"Touchdown, Purdue Pete!"

At halftime, the All-American
Marching Band performed on the field.

Purdue Pete and the crowd sang
Hail Purdue.

The Purdue Boilermakers
won the football game!

Purdue Pete gave the coach a
high-five. The coach said,
"Great game, Purdue Pete!"

After the football game, Purdue Pete
was tired. It had been a long day
at Purdue University.

He walked home and climbed into bed.

Goodnight, Purdue Pete.

For Anna and Maya,
and all of Purdue Pete's little fans. ~ AA

To all of the individuals who have portrayed Pete
over the years and to the Reynolds and Felton families;
especially Malik and Elijah. ~ JR

For more information about our products,
please visit us online at www.mascotbooks.com.

For information please contact Mascot Books,
P.O. Box 220157, Chantilly, VA 20153-0157.

PURDUE UNIVERSITY, BOILERMAKERS, PURDUE BOILERS, BOILERMAKER and
BOILERMAKER SPECIAL are trademarks or registered trademarks of Purdue
University and are used under license.

ISBN: 1-932888-30-6

Printed in the United States.

www.mascotbooks.com

Title List

Major League Baseball

Team	Title	Author
Boston Red Sox	Hello, *Wally*!	Jerry Remy
Boston Red Sox	*Wally The Green Monster* And His Journey Through *Red Sox Nation*!	Jerry Remy
Boston Red Sox	Coast to Coast with *Wally The Green Monster*	Jerry Remy
Boston Red Sox	A Season with *Wally The Green Monster*	Jerry Remy
Colorado Rockies	Hello, *Dinger*!	Aimee Aryal
Detroit Tigers	Hello, *Paws*!	Aimee Aryal
New York Yankees	Let's Go, *Yankees*!	Yogi Berra
New York Yankees	*Yankees Town*	Aimee Aryal
New York Mets	Hello, *Mr. Met*!	Rusty Staub
New York Mets	*Mr. Met* and his Journey Through the Big Apple	Aimee Aryal
St. Louis Cardinals	Hello, *Fredbird*!	Ozzie Smith
Philadelphia Phillies	Hello, *Phillie Phanatic*!	Aimee Aryal
Chicago Cubs	Let's Go, *Cubs*!	Aimee Aryal
Chicago White Sox	Let's Go, *White Sox*!	Aimee Aryal
Cleveland Indians	Hello, *Slider*!	Bob Feller
Seattle Mariners	Hello, *Mariner Moose*!	Aimee Aryal
Washington Nationals	Hello, *Screech*!	Aimee Aryal
Milwaukee Brewers	Hello, *Bernie Brewer*!	Aimee Aryal

College

School	Title	Author
Alabama	Hello, Big Al!	Aimee Aryal
Alabama	Roll Tide!	Ken Stabler
Alabama	Big Al's Journey Through the Yellowhammer State	Aimee Aryal
Arizona	Hello, Wilbur!	Lute Olson
Arkansas	Hello, Big Red!	Aimee Aryal
Arkansas	Big Red's Journey Through the Razorback State	Aimee Aryal
Auburn	Hello, Aubie!	Aimee Aryal
Auburn	War Eagle!	Pat Dye
Auburn	Aubie's Journey Through the Yellowhammer State	Aimee Aryal
Boston College	Hello, Baldwin!	Aimee Aryal
Brigham Young	Hello, Cosmo!	LaVell Edwards
Cal - Berkeley	Hello, Oski!	Aimee Aryal
Clemson	Hello, Tiger!	Aimee Aryal
Clemson	Tiger's Journey Through the Palmetto State	Aimee Aryal
Colorado	Hello, Ralphie!	Aimee Aryal
Connecticut	Hollo, Jonathan!	Aimee Aryal
Duke	Hello, Blue Devil!	Aimee Aryal
Florida	Hello, Albert!	Aimee Aryal
Florida State	Let's Go, 'Noles!	Aimee Aryal
Georgia	Hello, Hairy Dawg!	Aimee Aryal
Georgia	How 'Bout Them Dawgs!	Aimee Aryal
Georgia	Hairy Dawg's Journey Through the Peach State	Vince Dooley
Georgia Tech	Hello, Buzz!	Vince Dooley
Gonzaga	Spike, The Gonzaga Bulldog	Aimee Aryal / Mike Pringle
Illinois	Let's Go, Illini!	
Indiana	Let's Go, Hoosiers!	Aimee Aryal
Iowa	Hello, Herky!	Aimee Aryal
Iowa State	Hello, Cy!	Aimee Aryal
James Madison	Hello, Duke Dog!	Amy DeLashmutt
Kansas	Hello, Big Jay!	Aimee Aryal
Kansas State	Hello, Willie!	Aimee Aryal
Kentucky	Hello, Wildcat!	Dan Walter
LSU	Hello, Mike!	Aimee Aryal
LSU	Mike's Journey Through the Bayou State	Aimee Aryal
Maryland	Hello, Testudo!	Aimee Aryal
Michigan	Let's Go, Blue!	Aimee Aryal
Michigan State	Hello, Sparty!	Aimee Aryal
Minnesota	Hello, Goldy!	Aimee Aryal
Mississippi	Hello, Colonel Rebel!	Aimee Aryal
Mississippi State	Hello, Bully!	Aimee Aryal

Pro Football

Team	Title	Author
Carolina Panthers	Let's Go, Panthers!	Aimee Aryal
Chicago Bears	Let's Go, Bears!	Aimee Aryal
Dallas Cowboys	How 'Bout Them Cowboys!	Aimee Aryal
Green Bay Packers	Go, Pack, Go!	Aimee Aryal
Kansas City Chiefs	Let's Go, Chiefs!	Aimee Aryal
Minnesota Vikings	Let's Go, Vikings!	Aimee Aryal
New York Giants	Let's Go, Giants!	Aimee Aryal
New York Jets	J-E-T-S! Jets, Jets, Jets!	Aimee Aryal
New England Patriots	Let's Go, Patriots!	Aimee Aryal
Pittsburgh Steelers	Here We Go Steelers!	Aimee Aryal
Seattle Seahawks	Let's Go, Seahawks!	Aimee Aryal
Washington Redskins	Hail To The Redskins!	Aimee Aryal

Basketball

Team	Title	Author
Dallas Mavericks	Let's Go, Mavs!	Mark Cuban
Boston Celtics	Let's Go, Celtics!	Aimee Aryal

Other

Event	Title	Author
Kentucky Derby	White Diamond Runs For The Roses	Aimee Aryal
Marine Corps Marathon	Run, Miles, Run!	Aimee Aryal

School	Title	Author
Missouri	Hello, Truman!	Aimee Aryal
Nebraska	Hello, Herbie Husker!	Todd Donoh
North Carolina	Hello, Rameses!	Aimee Aryal
North Carolina	Rameses' Journey Through the Tar Heel State	Aimee Aryal
North Carolina St.	Hello, Mr. Wuf!	Aimee Aryal
North Carolina St.	Mr. Wuf's Journey Through North Carolina	Aimee Aryal
Notre Dame	Let's Go, Irish!	Aimee Aryal
Ohio State	Hello, Brutus!	Aimee Aryal
Ohio State	Brutus' Journey	Aimee Aryal
Oklahoma	Let's Go, Sooners!	Aimee Aryal
Oklahoma State	Hello, Pistol Pete!	Aimee Aryal
Oregon	Go Ducks!	Aimee Aryal
Oregon State	Hello, Benny the Beaver!	Aimee Aryal
Penn State	Hello, Nittany Lion!	Aimee Aryal
Penn State	We Are Penn State!	Aimee Aryal
Purdue	Hello, Purdue Pete!	Joe Paterno
Rutgers	Hello, Scarlet Knight!	Aimee Aryal
South Carolina	Hello, Cocky!	Aimee Aryal
South Carolina	Cocky's Journey Through the Palmetto State	Aimee Aryal
So. California	Hello, Tommy Trojan!	
Syracuse	Hello, Otto!	Aimee Aryal
Tennessee	Hello, Smokey!	Aimee Aryal
Tennessee	Smokey's Journey Through the Volunteer State	Aimee Aryal
Texas	Hello, Hook 'Em!	
Texas	Hook 'Em's Journey Through the Lone Star State	Aimee Aryal
Texas A & M	Howdy, Reveille!	
Texas A & M	Reveille's Journey Through the Lone Star State	Aimee Aryal
Texas Tech	Hello, Masked Rider!	
UCLA	Hello, Joe Bruin!	Aimee Aryal
Virginia	Hello, CavMan!	Aimee Aryal
Virginia Tech	Hello, Hokie Bird!	Aimee Aryal
Virginia Tech	Yea, It's Hokie Game Day!	Aimee Aryal
Virginia Tech	Hokie Bird's Journey Through Virginia	Frank Beam / Aimee Aryal
Wake Forest	Hello, Demon Deacon!	
Washington	Hello, Harry the Husky!	Aimee Aryal
Washington State	Hello, Butch!	Aimee Aryal
West Virginia	Hello, Mountaineer!	Aimee Aryal
Wisconsin	Hello, Bucky!	Aimee Aryal
Wisconsin	Bucky's Journey Through the Badger State	Aimee Aryal

Order online at **mascotbooks.com** using promo code " **free**" to receive **FREE SHIPPING!**

More great titles coming soon!

info@mascotbooks.com

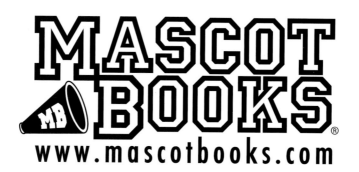
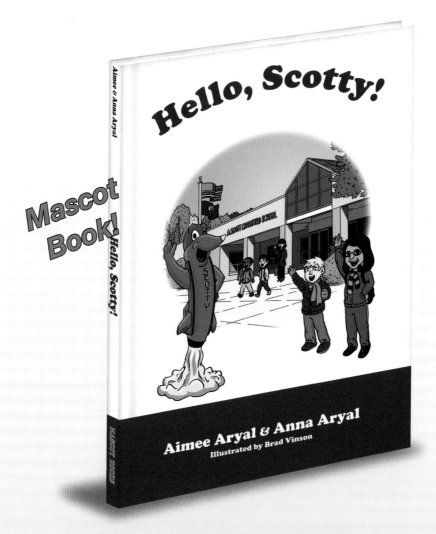

Let Mascot Books create a customized children's book for your school or team!

Here's how our fundraisers work ...

- Mascot Books creates a customized children's book with content specific to your school. When parents buy your school's book, your organization earns cash!

- When parents buy any of Mascot Books' college or professional team books, your organization earns more cash!

- We also offer options for a customized plush, apparel, and even mascot costumes!

Mascot Costumes!

Dougie the Dragon

Mascot T-Shirts!

Proud to be a Vincent Elementary Duck!

Vinny the Duck

Mascot Plush!

Lulu the Ladybug

For more information about the most innovative fundraiser on the market, contact us at info@mascotbooks.com.